Stancil

The King Who Rained

by FRED GWYNNE

Aladdin Paperbacks
New York   London   Toronto   Sydney

ALADDIN PAPERBACKS
An imprint of Simon & Schuster Children's Publishing Division
1230 Avenue of the Americas, New York, NY 10020
Originally published by Windmill Books, Inc. and Simon & Schuster, Inc.
ALADDIN PAPERBACKS, Stories to Go!, and colophon are trademarks of Simon & Schuster, Inc.
Manufactured in the United States of America
First Aladdin Paperbacks edition September 1987
First Aladdin Stories to Go! edition June 2006
10 9 8 7 6 5 4 3 2 1
The Library of Congress has cataloged the hardcover edition as follows:
Gwynne, Fred.
The king who rained.
SUMMARY: A little girl pictures the things her parents talk about, such as a king who rained, bear feet, and the foot prince in the snow.
English language—Homonyms—Juvenile literature. [1. English language—Homonyms] I. Title
PE1595-G75 1980 428.1 80-12939
ISBN-13: 978-0-671-96070-4 (hc.)
ISBN-10: 0-671-96070-9 (hc.)
ISBN-13: 978-0-671-66744-3 (Aladdin pbk.)
ISBN-10: 0-671-66744-0 (Aladdin pbk.)
ISBN-13: 978-1-4169-1858-5 (Stories to Go! pbk.)
ISBN-10: 1-4169-1858-2 (Stories to Go! pbk.)

P9-DML-589

To Madyn

Daddy says there was a king
who rained for forty years.

there are forks in the road.

Daddy says
he has a mole
on his nose.

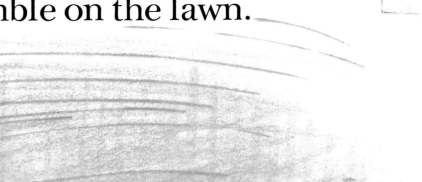

lambs gamble on the lawn.

Sometimes Mommy says she has a frog in her throat.

Other times she says she's
a little horse and
needs the throat spray.

And when I give it to her,
she says I'm a little deer.

My big sister's getting married
and she says I can hold up her train.

Daddy says next time he paints the house he's going to give it two coats.

Daddy says there's
a head on his beer.

Daddy says all we get
in the mail are big bills.

Mommy says not to bother

her when she's playing bridge.

Daddy says our family
has a coat of arms.

Daddy says we should
live in the present.

Mommy says little children
always have bear feet.

I've heard Daddy talk about the foot prince in the snow…

...and the blue prince for
the new room on our house.

Daddy says some boars
are coming to dinner.

Did you ever hear such a bunch of fairy tails?

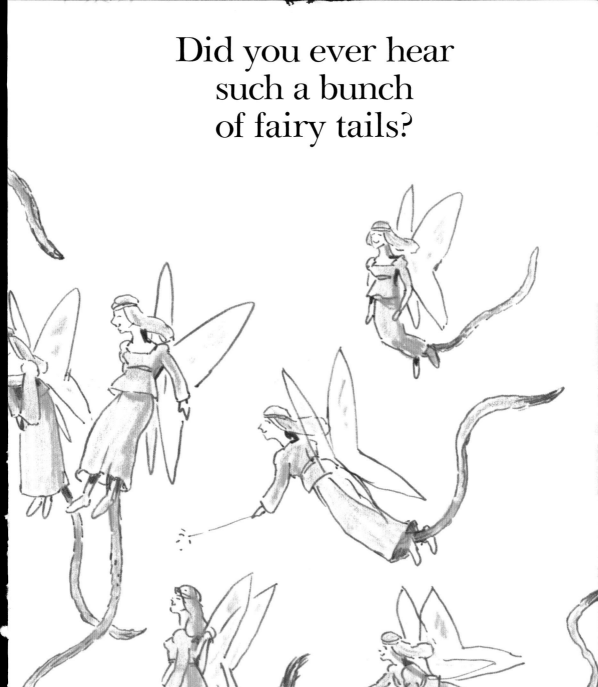